This book belongs to:

....

....

NO QUIZ

A catalogue record for this book is available from the British Library

Published by Ladybird Books Ltd
80 Strand London WC2R 0RL
A Penguin Company

2 4 6 8 10 9 7 5 3 1

© Ladybird Books Ltd MMVI

Endpaper map illustrations by Fred van Deelen

ISBN-13: 978-1-84646-064-7
ISBN-10: 1-84646-064-6

Printed in Italy

LADYBIRD TALES

The
Big Pancake

Retold by Vera Southgate M.A., B.Com

with illustrations by Andy Pritchett

Once upon a time, there was a mother who had seven little boys – seven, hungry, little boys.

One day, the mother began to make a very big pancake for her seven, hungry, little boys.

She took flour, salt, eggs and butter and mixed a batter.

Then she melted some butter in her biggest frying pan.

Then the mother poured the
batter into the big frying pan.
It made a very big pancake
– a huge pancake
– to feed seven, hungry, little boys.

The seven little boys watched the pancake as it cooked.

"We are hungry," they said. "Is the pancake ready yet?"

Their mother lifted up one side of the pancake and looked underneath.

"It is just turning golden," she said.

"Is it ready to eat?" asked the seven little boys.

"Oh, no!" said their mother, "I must toss it yet. I must toss it up in the air to turn it over, so that the other side will turn golden. Then it will be ready!"

"Oh dear!" thought the pancake. "I must not wait until my other side is golden or I shall be all eaten up by seven, hungry, little boys. And that will be the end of me! I will run away," thought the pancake. "Yes, I will run right away from seven, hungry, little boys."

The mother took the frying pan in both hands and tossed the pancake high in the air.

Then she held out the frying pan ready to catch the pancake as it turned in the air.

"Oh, no you don't!" said the pancake to itself. It gave a flip in the air, missed the frying pan and landed on the floor.

Then, with one side golden and the other side pale, it rolled away on its edge, like a very big penny.

The pancake rolled out of the door and away down the road.

"Stop!" shouted the mother, her frying pan still in her hand. "Stop!" she shouted, as she ran after the pancake.

Faster and faster rolled the pancake, away down the road.

The seven, hungry, little boys ran down the road behind their mother.

"Stop!" they shouted. "We want to eat you!"

"Oh, no!" said the pancake as it rolled on, faster and faster. "I don't want to be eaten by seven, hungry, little boys."

Soon the pancake passed a man.

"Stop!" shouted the man.
"You look like a delicious pancake.
Please let me eat you."

"Oh, no!" said the pancake.
"I don't want to be eaten.
A mother couldn't catch me.
Seven little boys couldn't catch me.
And I won't let *you* catch me!"

Then the pancake rolled on, faster and faster.

The man joined in behind the seven, hungry, little boys and the mother. And they all ran after the big pancake.

Soon the pancake passed a cat.

"Stop!" shouted the cat.
"You look like a delicious pancake.
Please let me eat you."

"Oh, no!" said the pancake.
"I don't want to be eaten.
A mother couldn't catch me.
Seven little boys couldn't catch me.
A man couldn't catch me.
And I won't let *you* catch me!"

Then the pancake rolled on, faster and faster.

The cat joined in behind the man and the seven, hungry, little boys and the mother.

And they all ran after the big pancake.

Soon the pancake passed
a cockerel.

"Stop!" shouted the cockerel.
"You look like a delicious pancake.
Please let me eat you."

"Oh, no!" said the pancake.
"I don't want to be eaten.
A mother couldn't catch me.
Seven little boys couldn't catch me.
A man couldn't catch me.
A cat couldn't catch me.
And I won't let *you* catch me!"

Then the pancake rolled on,
faster and faster.

The cockerel joined in behind
the cat and the man and the seven,
hungry, little boys and the mother.

And they all ran after the
big pancake.

Soon the pancake passed a duck.

"Stop!" shouted the duck.
"You look like a delicious pancake.
Please let me eat you."

"Oh, no!" said the pancake.
"I don't want to be eaten.
A mother couldn't catch me.
Seven little boys couldn't catch me.
A man couldn't catch me.
A cat couldn't catch me.
A cockerel couldn't catch me.
And I won't let *you* catch me!"

Then the pancake rolled on,
faster and faster.

The duck joined in behind the
cockerel and the cat and the man
and the seven, hungry, little boys
and the mother.

And they all ran after the
big pancake.

Soon the pancake passed a cow.

"Stop!" shouted the cow.
"You look like a delicious pancake.
Please let me eat you."

"Oh, no!" said the pancake.
"I don't want to be eaten.
A mother couldn't catch me.
Seven little boys couldn't catch me.
A man couldn't catch me.
A cat couldn't catch me.
A cockerel couldn't catch me.
A duck couldn't catch me.
And I won't let *you* catch me!"

Then the pancake rolled on,
faster and faster. The cow joined
in behind the duck and the cockerel
and the cat and the man and the
seven, hungry, little boys and the
mother. And they all ran after the
big pancake.

Soon the pancake passed a pig.

"Where are you going in such a hurry?" asked the pig.

"I am running away from a mother, seven, hungry, little boys, a man, a cat, a cockerel, a duck and a cow," said the big pancake. "They all want to eat me and I don't want to be eaten up."

"Of course you don't want to be eaten up!" said the pig, as he ran along beside the pancake. "I never heard of such a thing!"

Soon the pancake and the pig came to a river.

"Now, what am I going to do?" the pancake asked the pig. "I can't swim!"

"But I can swim," said the pig.
"You get on my snout and I'll take
you across the river."
So the pancake rolled onto the
pig's snout. Then the pig opened
his mouth and gobbled up
the pancake.

And it *was* a delicious pancake!

That was the end of the
big pancake.

So the mother and the seven
hungry, little boys and the man
and the cat and the cockerel and
the duck and the cow never *did*
catch the big pancake!